FLOODS

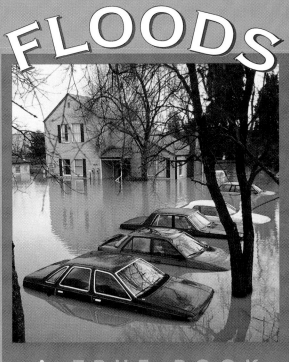

A TRUE BOOK

by

**Paul P. and
Diane M. Sipiera**

Children's Press®
A Division of Grolier Publishing

New York London Hong Kong Sydney
Danbury, Connecticut

Reading Consultant
Linda Cornwell
Learning Resource Consultant
Indiana Department
of Education

Author's Dedication
To those who helped us repair
our Galena home after the
1993 flood

A stop sign almost
under floodwaters

Visit Children's Press® on the Internet at:
http://publishing.grolier.com

Library of Congress Cataloging-in-Publication Data

Sipiera, Paul P.
    Floods / by Paul P. and Diane M. Sipiera.
        p.   cm. — (A true book)
    Includes bibliographical references and index.
    Summary: Explains the importance of water to life on Earth, how
flooding occurs, and some of its most devastating consequences.
    ISBN: 0-516-20668-0 (lib.bdg.)   0-516-26434-6 (pbk.)
    1. Floods—Juvenile literature. [1. Floods.] I. Sipiera, Diane M. II. Title.
III. Series.
GB1399.S56   1998
551.48'9—dc21   97-28536
                                                                 CIP
                                                                 AC

Contents

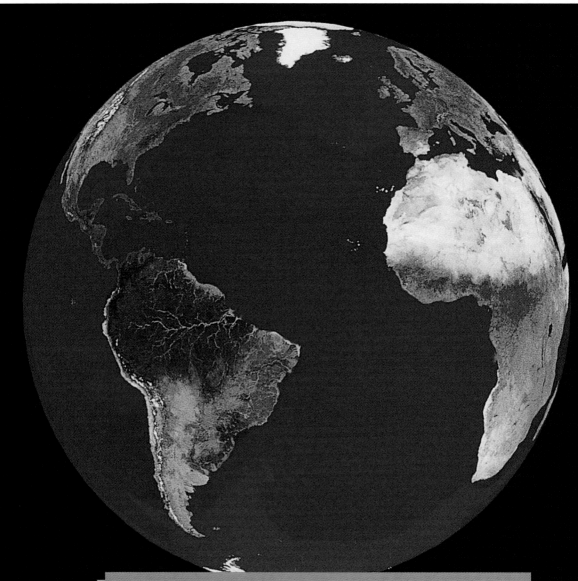

This partial view of Earth shows that water (shown in blue) covers most of our planet.

The Water Planet

On Earth, water is everywhere. From the smallest pond to the frozen ice sheet of Antarctica, water plays an important role. The oceans of the world cover much of Earth's surface. From space, water makes Earth look like a blue planet.

The world's oceans are always moving. You can see

You can watch the movement of Earth's water anytime you visit an ocean or lake.

waves move across the surface of the ocean. When you are at the beach, you can watch waves wash up on shore. Even lakes have small waves. Sometimes, an earthquake causes huge waves called tsunamis (tsoo-NAH-meez) to form. When these waves reach shore, they can wash away everything in their path.

Powerful wind and rain storms, such as hurricanes or typhoons, can do the same

A typhoon in Tahiti, an island in the South Pacific

thing. Although the oceans can cause great damage, they are important to life on Earth.

One of the most powerful forces in nature is running water. Water wears away Earth's surface. Over very long periods of time, running water can destroy huge mountains. It can also cut deep canyons. It has taken about six million years for the Colorado River to form the

The Colorado River has spent millions of years carving the Grand Canyon.

Grand Canyon of Arizona. Great mountains such as the Rockies in the western United States will someday be worn down. But that will not happen for millions of years.

Where Does Water Come From?

The water that we see today formed long ago when Earth was young. Most of this water can be found in the oceans. But there is water in the air and on land, too. Water moves from the oceans, to the air, and onto the land. This movement is

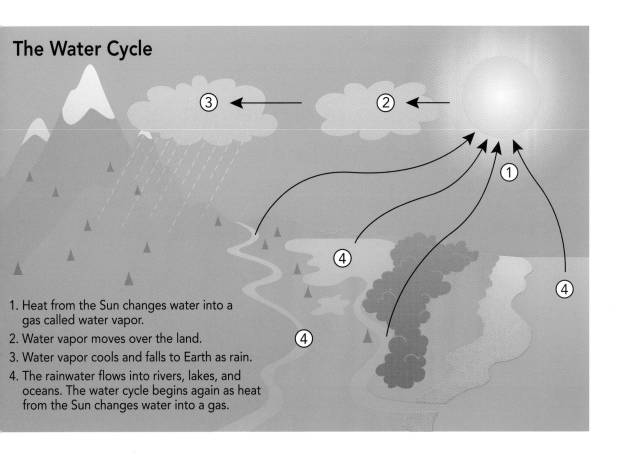

The Water Cycle

1. Heat from the Sun changes water into a gas called water vapor.
2. Water vapor moves over the land.
3. Water vapor cools and falls to Earth as rain.
4. The rainwater flows into rivers, lakes, and oceans. The water cycle begins again as heat from the Sun changes water into a gas.

called the water cycle. Heat from the Sun changes water from the oceans into a gas. This warm, moist gas moves over the land. It cools slowly and then turns into rain. The rain falls to the ground. Some of the rain falls into lakes. Some of it goes into rivers. The rivers take the rain back into the oceans. And the water cycle begins again with the Sun's heat.

The water cycle does not work exactly the same way everywhere on Earth. Temperatures are hot near the equator (the imaginary line around the middle of the earth, halfway between the North and South

Rain forests near the equator thrive because it rains often there.

Poles). As a result, large amounts of water are changed into a gas. Because of this, it rains a lot in the areas near the equator.

Near the North Pole and South Pole, there is little heat. The Sun cannot change much water into gas. Without moist air, there is not much rain. This is why there is little rainfall at the North or South Pole—even in the summer. Desert areas of the earth do not have much water, either. As a result, it doesn't rain often. However, most of the earth has a mixture of both rainy and dry days.

Antarctica, near the South Pole, (above) and desert regions (right) are two areas of Earth that do not receive much rain.

Too Much Water

The amount of rain that falls can be either good or bad. In the regions of the world where food is grown, farmers hope for just the right amount of rain. If there is too much sunshine and not enough rain, crops will die. The same is true for too much rain. When

Rain is important for crops, such as wheat, to grow.

there is too much rain all at once, crops will rot in the fields or wash away. Some

Rice grows in water-covered fields called paddies.

crops, such as rice, need large amounts of water. But even rice needs to have sunshine.

When it rains hard for long periods of time, the ground becomes soaked with water. Soon the ground can't hold any more. Water then quickly flows down hills and over the

Puddles of water may remain after heavy rains because the ground could not soak up the water fast enough.

ground. This is called runoff water. Plants are either washed away or drowned. This type of flooding may not affect a large area, but it can cause serious damage to farms.

When heavy rains continue over a large area, the water will begin to collect in small streams. These streams flow into larger rivers. If a river gets too much water, it will overflow. When this happens,

Heavy rains can cause streams and rivers to overflow.

This man is using a small boat and a guide rope to reach safety after his home was flooded.

the river becomes much wider than usual. The flooding river can damage the homes and property of the people who live nearby. It can be dangerous for people to remain there. Sometimes people must leave their homes until the danger has passed.

Even small rivers, or streams, can have severe floods. People who live near these small rivers sometimes see their homes ruined by the floodwaters of a normally peaceful stream.

Dangerous Floods

Floods can be dangerous no matter where you live. It is usually safe to swim in a river. But when a river is flooding, it is flowing very fast. Even excellent swimmers can be caught in its strong current. The force of floodwater is quite powerful.

Floodwater carried this house down a mountainside in Washington State.

Big trees and even houses can be carried away by a flooded river.

After heavy rainfall high in the mountains, or in the spring when the snow melts, water quickly flows downhill. This can produce a giant wall of water. The force of the water can push huge rocks around as if they were little pebbles. As the water rushes away from the mountains, it spreads out over flat land. It can quickly fill dried-out riverbeds or small canyons. Anyone caught in these low areas when the

This flash flood is occurring in Sulphur Creek in Spring Capitol Reef National Park, Utah.

water comes through will be in danger of drowning. This kind of flood is called a flash flood.

Flooding in downtown Richmond, Virginia, after the James River flooded the city

Flash floods were once thought to be dangerous only in mountainous areas. But flash floods can occur in large cities. There, much of the ground is covered by concrete and asphalt. During a heavy rain-storm, the water cannot soak into the ground. Cities have sewers to collect the rainwater underground. If the city's sew-ers can't hold all of this water, the water will flood people's homes and businesses.

Basements can become filled with dirty water. This dirty water may contain germs that make people sick.

Sometimes, cars and trucks on flooded streets become completely surrounded by water. If the water gets into the engine of a car or a truck, these vehicles won't work. If the water is high enough to reach the engine of a vehicle, it is too dangerous for any-one to walk through. People

Drivers stranded in floodwaters on an Argentina highway

who get stuck in their cars or trucks should wait patiently until help arrives.

Another kind of flood occurs when a dam breaks. Dams are structures that hold back the water of a stream or river. Often, people live in valleys below the dam. But this can be a dangerous place to build a home. If the dam breaks, a flood of water will roar down the valley. The water travels very fast, destroying everything in its path. Sometimes it happens so fast that people don't have time to reach safety.

The Glen Canyon Dam
on the Colorado River
in Page, Arizona

Although this is a carefully controlled dam break, this photo shows how powerful rushing water can be.

Many people who have been killed by floods were victims of a dam break.

Spring Floods

Each spring, many of the world's rivers flood. This is because of melting winter snow and heavy spring rains. When the rivers reach their highest levels, they have reached their crest. After a river crests, the floodwaters will slowly move back to the river. The water is gone, but huge

Residents of Malibu, California, shovel the mud left behind from flooding that occurred in January 1995.

amounts of mud and silt are left behind. Everything is a big mess.

In spite of flooding, people still choose to live near rivers. The land near a river is usually rich farmland. Many communities try to protect themselves from

Helpful Floods

Ancient people who lived in Egypt depended on flooding to grow their food. Each summer, they waited for the Nile River to overflow before planting their crops. They also used the floodwaters to supply water to fields that were far from the river. Floods also carried rich soil to the land near the river. Since crops grow well in rich soil, the people looked forward to good crops almost every year.

Townspeople in St. Charles, Missouri, build a sandbag levee across a street in 1993 to hold back the floodwaters of the Missouri River.

floods by building levees. Levees are banks that are built along a river to prevent flooding. Levees are often built by filling large bags with sand and piling them on top of each other.

An Endless Cycle

As you have seen, floods can be both good and bad. A good flood provides rich soil and water for farming areas. But when a flood threatens people's lives and land, it is a great danger. Safety measures must be taken to protect the people who live near rivers.

Family members in Kaskaskia, Illinois, comfort each other after being forced to leave their home before floodwaters arrive in July 1993.

Levees and dams can control the harsh effects of flooding. But floods can not always be controlled. They are just part of the way nature works.

The owners of some of the houses in this neighborhood have placed sandbags around their homes to try to keep the water out.

There will always be flooding. People must find ways to remain safe and to protect their property.

Flood Facts

The light brown areas mark where a flash flood occurred in this desert region.

Flash floods can occur in the desert. Water that melts high up in the mountains can rush with great force into the dry, desert areas below. It is always wise to avoid camping or hiking in low areas of the desert.

Beavers can cause floods. Beavers build their dens by blocking, or damming, small streams. As a result, water can overflow the banks of the stream and cause small floods.

As this beaver builds his den, he is really building a dam across the stream.

Chicago's underground tunnels hold rainwater, but sometimes the hoses that pump out the water leak. This causes more flooding!

Chicago, Illinois, has problems with flooding. When it rains heavily in Chicago, there isn't enough ground to soak up the water. The city has built a huge underground system of tunnels to hold rainwater until it can be safely pumped out.

To Find Out More

Here are some additional resources to help you learn more about floods:

 **Books**

Calhoun, Mary. **Flood!** Morrow, 1997.

Ganeri. Anita. **Weather.** Franklin Watts, 1993.

Kerr, Daisy. **Ancient Egyptians.** Franklin Watts, 1996.

Morris, Neil. **Rivers.** Raintree Steck-Vaughn, 1997.

Murray, Peter. **Floods.** Child's World, 1996.

Palmer, Joy. **Rain.** Raintree Steck-Vaughn, 1992.

Organizations and Online Sites

American Red Cross
http://www.redcross.org

The American Red Cross is a service organization that provides relief to victims of disasters. The Red Cross also helps people to prevent, prepare for, and respond to emergencies. The Red Cross web site contains a dictionary of disaster-related words, a disaster I.Q. test, and links to other sites.

National Aeronautics and Space Adminstration (NASA)
http://ltwww.gsfc.nasa.gov/ndrd/disaster (Keyword: Flood)

This site contains information about floods and links to sites related to specific floods, including how to prepare for flooding and how to tell if a flash flood might occur.

Federal Emergency Management Agency (FEMA)
Federal Center Plaza
500 C. Street, S.W.
Washington, DC 20472
http://www.fema.gov/

Important Words

canyon deep narrow river valley with steep sides

crops grains such as wheat, corn, or beans that are grown for food

current the movement of water in a river or ocean

nature everything in the world that is not made by people, such as plants, animals, and the weather

riverbank the high ground on either side of a river

silt fine sand and mud that is carried along by a river

Index

Meet the Authors

Paul and Diane Sipiera are husband and wife who share a common interest in science and nature. Paul is a college professor in Palatine, Illinois. Diane is the director of education for the Planetary Studies Foundation of Algonquin, Illinois. Together with their daughters Andrea, Paula, and Carrie Ann, the Sipieras enjoy their little farm in Galena, Illinois.